Text copyright © 2020 by Aimée Bissonette
Illustrations copyright © 2020 by Kelly Pousette

Book design by Melissa Nelson Greenberg

Library of Congress Cataloging-in-Publication Data available.
ISBN: 978-1-944903-85-5

Printed in China.

10 9 8 7 6 5 4 3 2 1

Cameron Kids is an imprint of Cameron + Company

Cameron + Company
Petaluma, California
www.cameronbooks.com

With all my love to Bryan, Aliza, Maureen, and Brian.
Things don't always go as planned,
but we always have each other—and that's all I ever need!
—A.B.

For my mum and sister, who both love gardens and party dresses.
—K.P.

Do Not Rake Your Garden in a Party Dress

by Aimée Bissonette

illustrated by Kelly Pousette

cameron kids

When you've invited your friends for a tea party at two,
pinned up your hair and polished your shoes,
planned the music, the seating, the menu just so . . .

Do not rake your garden in a party dress.

For if you do . . .
a great spring wind might catch you up
and send you soaring —

WHOOSH!—

loop-dee-looping
to the clouds until
your house is just a tiny speck below.

And a passing eagle might come to fetch you
and carry you to its nest of sticks and grass,
dropping you —

PLOP!—

onto a bed of fine feathers
next to a pair of eaglet chicks.

And those fuzzy eaglets might press up warm against you,
making you giggle as they wriggle,
their fuzzy feathers in your face until —

aH-CHOO!—

and you just might topple from that fine, fine nest . . .

And tumble, bumble downward
until you catch an outstretched limb
and swing from sunlight into shade,
sweet birdsong all around you until —

SNAP!

But worry not, you'll put that party dress to work
and find that you are floating,
your party dress a perfect parachute,
floating, floating until —

SPLaSH!—

you're in the lake among a family of otters,
who tickle, twirl, and toss you as they swim to the far shore . . .

Where you'll wiggle away and wade out of the water,
dripping, drenched, and dizzy.
"Such a kerfuffle!" you'll say as you wring water from your dress.
Then you'll march home, your soggy shoes

SQUISH, SQUISH, SQUISHING

as you go.

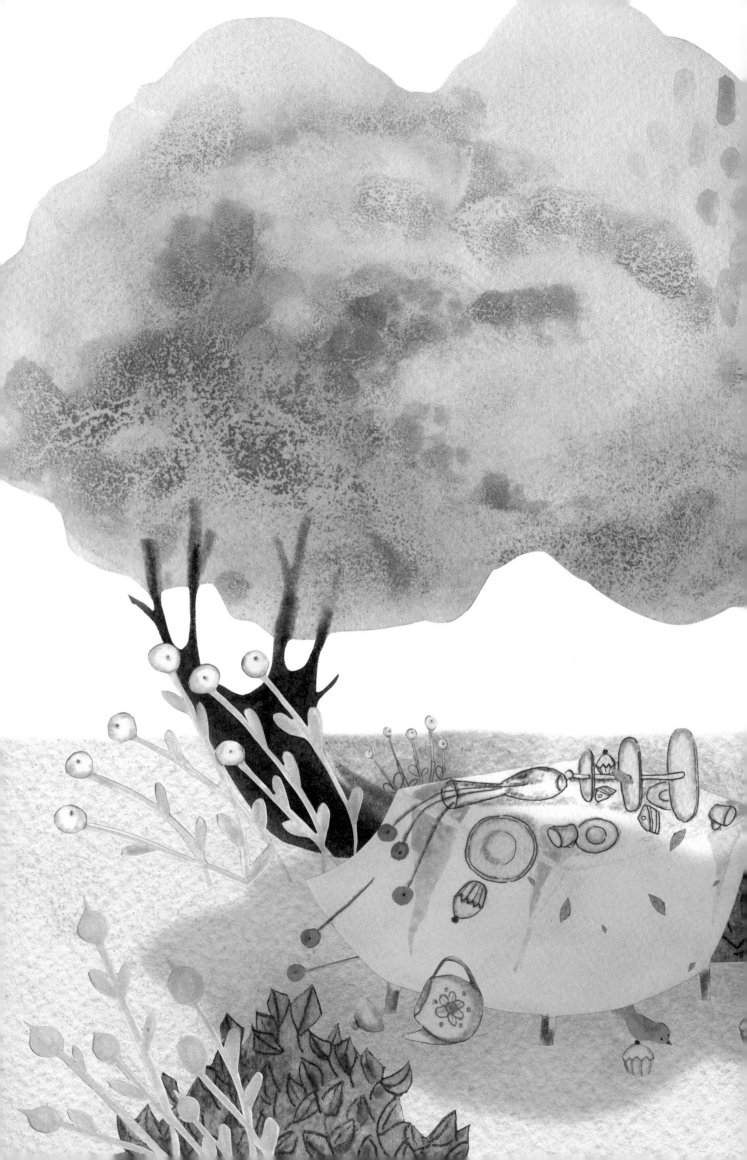

And when at last you're back at home,
wild, wet, and windswept,
you'll go inside to change your clothes,
because — it's nearly two o'clock! —
your guests will be arriving soon and . . .

your garden still needs raking.

This time, you'll set your party dress aside
and put on a proper pair of overalls,
       a kerchief,
              and boots.

And this you will know —

things don't always go as planned . . .

Which just might make for a better party after all!